D1500964

Percy Trezise AM was an Australian pilot, painter, explorer and writer as well as a documenter and historian of Aboriginal rock art. For many years, he worked closely with Aboriginal author and artist Dick Roughsey, with whom he collaborated on picture books for children, retelling legends and stories drawn from Aboriginal oral history. In 1996 he was made a member of the Order of Australia, and in 2004 he was awarded an Honorary Doctorate of Letters by James Cook University.

Angus&Robertson
An imprint of HarperCollins*Children'sBooks*, Australia

First published in Australia in 1987
by William Collins Pty Limited
This edition published in 2015
by HarperCollins*Publishers* Australia Pty Limited
ABN 36 009 913 517
harpercollins.com.au

HarperCollins*Publishers*
Level 13, 201 Elizabeth Street, Sydney NSW 2000, Australia
Unit D1, 63 Apollo Drive, Rosedale, Auckland 0632, New Zealand
A 53, Sector 57, Noida, UP, India
1 London Bridge Street, London, SE1 9GF, United Kingdom
2 Bloor Street East, 20th floor, Toronto, Ontario M4W 1A8, Canada
195 Broadway, New York NY 10007, USA

National Library of Australia Cataloguing-in-Publication data:

Trezise, P.J. (Percy J.).
The owl people
ISBN 978 0 2071 7703 3 (pbk.)
1. Aborigines, Australian – Legends – Juvenile literature.
I. Title.
398.20994

Colour reproduction by Graphic Print Group, Adelaide, South Australia
Printed and bound in China by RR Donnelley

6 5 4 3 2 18

The Owl People

PERCY TREZISE

Angus&Robertson
An imprint of HarperCollins*Children'sBooks*

The white-faced owl and the red mopoke owl were brothers.
With their two sisters they were travellling north looking for their
grandmother, the old Mopoke woman.

The Owl People were cannibals and as they travelled they hunted and killed people for food. On a bank of the Palmer River they found a fresh camp, where the ashes were still warm in the fireplaces.

The Owl People looked about for tracks and followed them until they saw a young man running ahead. It was Alpudda, the coucal, and he was nice and fat, so the Owl brothers chased and speared him.

The Owl sisters cut bark and made bark vessels to cook Alpudda, while their brothers got firewood and stones to heat for a ground oven.

They cut Alpudda up and put the pieces of meat in the bark vessels and added water and hot stones. Then they put them in a pit with hot stones, covered them over with large sheets of paperbark and heaped stones over the bark.

When the meat was cooked they found there was a lot of soup with it, so they made wads of fine soft grass and sat around mopping up the soup and eating it. They hung the meat in a tree for next day.

The Owl People found their Mopoke grandmother camped further along the Palmer River. She was boss of a big dog — as big as a bullock! This big dog had a small pup.

The Owl girls went to get bark to build huts, while the Owl brothers went with their grandmother and her monster dogs to hunt for more men.

The Owl hunting party found a camp with bark shades and fires still burning. Spears and food baskets were lying about as though the people had left suddenly.

Old Granny Mopoke sooled her dog along the tracks of the people.
The ground shook and thundered as it galloped after them.

The running people could hear the monster dog howling as it thundered after them. Women and children hid in hollow logs, while the men ran on to lead the dog away.

One man tripped and fell and the savage monster dog pounced on him. The rest of the men ran away yelling, "Yackai, yackai, yackai."

While this was happening, the pup ran into another camp and attacked Jimbal, the tree goanna, and Andidjeri, the sugar glider. Jimbal kicked the pup, knocking it over, and the pup ran away howling.

Jimbal and Andidjeri knew the pup would soon come back with the big dog. They decided to make a boggy place so the big dog would get stuck, then they could spear it.

Jimbal and Andidjeri painted themselves for the rain-making ceremony. They then threw their magic quartz crystals up in the air, singing and running around a circle.

The magic rain fell but only in the circle. They ran about thrusting their spears into the ground to make it soft and boggy. When the bog was made they gathered lots of spears and a big stone axe. Now they were ready to kill the monster dog.

The men heard the dog coming when it was still far off; it was howling as it came. They each fitted a spear into their woomeras and stood waiting on the far side of the bog.

Suddenly the big dog came galloping over the ridge in front of them.
It saw Jimbal and Andidjeri and rushed at them, howling horribly.

The monster dog hit the mud with a mighty splash and began to sink in it. Andidjeri ran around to the other side. Both men began to spear it, one from each side.

Jimbal sang out as he threw spears saying, "When it bogs belly-deep I'll jump on its back and smash its head with the axe. Don't you hit me with a spear."

They kept hurling spears into the howling monster as it sank deeper in the bog. Then Jimbal grabbed the stone axe, ran along the dog's tail and up on to its back. He began smashing it on the head.

After a long battle they finally killed the big dog. Jimbal and Andidjeri went back to their camp for food and water, and a rest after their hard work.

In the evening they came back with other men and dragged the big dog out of the bog. They cut its body into small pieces and hurled it all over the country.

The pieces of the monster dog turned into small dingoes which are always friendly to people. From that time people have had dingoes to help them hunt kangaroos and other animals.

Jimbal and Andidjeri left the other men cutting up the big dog. Now that it was dead they decided to try and get rid of the cannibal Owl People.

They found the Owl People in a lily lagoon, and crept up through the grass. Jimbal and Andidjeri leapt out of the grass and speared the Owl brothers.

They chased and caught the two Owl girls and went to the Owl People's camp. They speared the old Mopoke woman and the pup of the monster dog.

Jimbal and Andidjeri then decided to take the Owl girls with them and travel back to their own country far to the north.